The
Three Little Wolves
and the
Big Bad Pig

EUGENE TRIVIZAS
ILLUSTRATED BY HELEN OXENBURY

ALADDIN PAPERBACKS

For Grace
E. T.

In Memory of
Stanley
H. O.

ALADDIN PAPERBACKS
An imprint of Simon & Schuster Children's Publishing Division
1230 Avenue of the Americas, New York, NY 10020
Text copyright © 1993 by Eugene Trivizas
Illustrations copyright © 1993 by Helen Oxenbury
First published 1993 by Heinemann Young Books, part of
Reed International Books Limited, London, England.
Also available in a Margaret K. McElderry hardcover edition.

Manufactured in Singapore

1209 TWP

15

The Library of Congress has cataloged the hardcover edition as follows:
Trivizas, Eugene.
The three little wolves and the big bad pig / by Eugene Trivizas;
illustrated by Helen Oxenbury. —1st United States ed.
p. cm.
Summary: An altered retelling of the traditional tale about the conflict
between pig and wolf—with a surprise ending.
ISBN-13: 978-0-689-50569-0 (ISBN-10: 0-689-50569-8) (hc.)
[1. Folklore.] I. Oxenbury, Helen, ill. II. Title: 3 little wolves and the big bad pig.
PZ8.1.T7384Th 1993
398.24'52—dc20 92-24829

ISBN-13: 978-0-689-81528-7 (ISBN-10: 0-689-81528-X) (Aladdin pbk.)

Once upon a time, there were three cuddly little wolves with soft fur and fluffy tails who lived with their mother. The first was black, the second was gray, and the third was white.

One day the mother called the three little wolves around her and said, "My children, it is time for you to go out into the world. Go and build a house for yourselves. But beware of the big bad pig."

"Don't worry, Mother, we will watch out for him," said the three little wolves, and they set off.

Soon they met a kangaroo who was pushing a
wheelbarrow full of red and yellow bricks.
"Please, will you give us some
of your bricks?" asked
the three little wolves.

"Certainly," said the kangaroo, and she gave them
lots of red and yellow bricks.
So the three little wolves built themselves a
house of bricks.

The very next day the big bad pig came
prowling down the road and saw
the house of bricks that the
little wolves had built.
The three little wolves were
playing croquet in the garden.
When they saw the big bad pig coming,
they ran inside the house and locked the door.

The pig knocked on the door and grunted,
"Little wolves, little wolves, let me come in!"

"No, no, no," said the three little wolves. "By the
hair on our chinny-chin-chins, we will not let you
in, not for all the tea leaves in our china teapot!"

"Then I'll huff and I'll puff and I'll blow your house down!" said the pig.

So he huffed and he puffed and he puffed and he huffed, but the house didn't fall down.

But the pig wasn't called big and bad for nothing.
He went and fetched his sledgehammer, and he
knocked the house down.

The three little wolves
only just managed to escape before the bricks
crumbled, and they were very frightened indeed.

"We shall have to build a stronger house," they said.
Just then they saw a beaver who was mixing
concrete in a concrete mixer.

"Please, will you give us some of your concrete?"
asked the three little wolves.

"Certainly," said the beaver, and he gave them buckets and buckets full of messy, slurry concrete.

So the three little wolves built themselves a house of concrete.

No sooner had they finished than the big bad pig came prowling down the road and saw the house of concrete that the little wolves had built.

They were playing battledore and shuttlecock in the garden, and when they saw the big bad pig coming, they ran inside their house and shut the door.

The pig rang the bell and said, "Little frightened wolves, let me come in!"

"No, no, no," said the three little wolves. "By the hair on our chinny-chin-chins, we will not let you in, not for all the tea leaves in our china teapot."

"Then I'll huff and I'll puff and I'll blow your house down!" said the pig.

So he huffed and he puffed and he puffed and he huffed, but the house didn't fall down.

But the pig wasn't called big and bad for nothing.
He went and fetched his pneumatic drill and
smashed the house down.

The three little wolves
managed to escape, but their chinny-chin-chins were
trembling and trembling and trembling.

"We shall build an even stronger house," they said, because they were very determined. Just then they saw a truck coming along the road carrying barbed wire, iron bars, armor plates, and heavy metal padlocks.

"Please, will you give us some of your barbed wire, a few iron bars and armor plates, and some heavy metal padlocks?" they said to the rhinoceros who was driving the truck.

"Sure," said the rhinoceros, and he gave them plenty of barbed wire, iron bars, armor plates, and heavy metal padlocks. He also gave them some Plexiglas and some reinforced steel chains, because he was a generous and kindhearted rhinoceros.

So the three little wolves built themselves an extremely strong house. It was the strongest, securest house one could possibly imagine. They felt absolutely safe.

The next day the big bad pig came prowling along
the road as usual. The three little wolves were playing
hopscotch in the garden. When they saw the big bad
pig coming, they ran inside their house, bolted the
door, and locked all the thirty-seven padlocks.

The pig dialed the video entrance phone and said,
"Little frightened wolves with the trembling chins,
let me come in!"

"No, no, no!" said the little wolves. "By the hair on our chinny-chin-chins, we will not let you in, not for all the tea leaves in our china teapot."

"Then I'll huff and I'll puff and I'll blow your house down!" said the pig.

So he huffed and he puffed and he puffed and he huffed, but the house didn't fall down. But the pig wasn't called big and bad for nothing. He brought some dynamite, laid it against the house, lit the fuse, and...

the house
blew up.

The three little wolves
just managed to escape
with their fluffy tails scorched.

"Something must be wrong with our building materials," they said. "We have to try something different. But *what*?"

At that moment they saw a flamingo coming along pushing a wheelbarrow full of flowers.

"Please, will you give us some flowers?" asked the little wolves.

"With pleasure," said the flamingo, and he gave them lots of flowers. So the three little wolves built themselves a house of flowers.

One wall was of marigolds, one of daffodils, one of pink roses, and one of cherry blossoms. The ceiling was made of sunflowers, and the floor was a carpet of daisies. They had water lilies in their bathtub, and buttercups in their refrigerator. It was a rather fragile house and it swayed in the wind, but it was very beautiful.

Next day the big bad pig came prowling down the road and saw the house of flowers that the three little wolves had built.

He rang the bluebell at the door and said, "Little frightened wolves with the trembling chins and the scorched tails, let me come in!"

"No, no, no," said the three little wolves. "By the hair on our chinny-chin-chins, we will not let you in, not for all the tea leaves in our china teapot!"

"Then I'll huff and I'll puff and I'll blow your house down!" said the pig.

But as he took a deep breath, ready to huff and puff, he smelled the soft scent of the flowers. It was fantastic. And because the scent was so lovely, the pig took another breath and then another. Instead of huffing and puffing, he began to sniff.

He sniffed deeper and deeper until he was quite filled with the fragrant scent. His heart grew tender, and he realized how horrible he had been. Right then he decided to become a big *good* pig.
He started to sing and to dance the tarantella.

At first the three little wolves were a bit worried. It might be a trick. But soon they realized that the pig had truly changed, so they came running out of the house.

They started playing games with him.

First they played pig-pog and then piggy-in-the-middle,
and when they were all tired, they
invited him into the house.

They offered him tea and strawberries
and wolfberries, and asked him to stay with
them as long as he wanted.
The pig accepted, and they all lived happily
together ever after.